A muddy, soggy, smelly
monster comes struggling
out of the pond.

A silly, happy, jolly monster is doing handstands in the park.

A cuddly, fluffy, sleepy monster - will he ever get out of bed?

A speedy, sporty, spotty monster
runs quickly up the street.

A silver, sparkly, glittering monster is having...

...a monster party!

Monster party, fun for all,
Monsters run out from the hall.

There they are, monsters all,
Noisy monsters shout and call.

Monster party, fun for all,
That clever monster is dribbling
a ball.

There they are, monsters all,
Tumbling monsters, big and small.

There they are, monsters all,
Quick, that monster is
about to fall.

There they are, monsters all,
It is lucky that monster is long
and tall.

The monster party was fun for all,

Sh!

Sleeping monsters against the wall.